WILDLIFE TALES

Bear Rescue!

by Maria Rosado
illustrated by the Thompson Bros.

SCHOLASTIC INC.

New York   Toronto   London   Auckland   Sydney
Mexico City   New Delhi   Hong Kong   Buenos Aires

Chapter 1

"And . . . action!" Mom yelled.

With a sigh I adjusted my wing and waddled away from my burrow in the dunes. "Awwwrrr! Awrrrrr! Awrrrawrrr!" I called out, which means "Mommy! Daddy! Where are you?" In penguin, that is.

"Cut!"

Mom popped out from behind the big video monitor on the nearby boardwalk. The monitor was displaying the view from a remote camera mounted on my head.

"Honey, I know it was just a rehearsal, but—," Mom started to say.

"Like, that stunk," Debbie interrupted. "Big time." Debbie's my sister. She doesn't even speak penguin, but that didn't stop her from criticizing my performance.

It's hard for my dad to criticize anybody. So he smiled at me and said, "But

3

your waddle was smashing, poppet!"

I could see Mom was trying to be patient. "Eliza, do you think you could give it a little more feeling this time?"

I just groaned. It wasn't easy being a penguin.

See, Dad hosts *Nigel Thornberry's Animal World* and Mom films it. It was because of Dad's show that we were here in Australia, and I was dressed up in a penguin suit.

At sunset, tons of penguin parents were due on that very beach. My best friend Darwin—who is a chimpanzee—and I were the only ones small enough to move among the birds and not alarm them. Well, Donnie is also small enough to have done it, but there was no telling what *else* he might do.

Donnie came to live with us after we found him living alone in the jungle in Borneo. It *is* understandable, but at times he acts more like the wild animals we film than like a little boy. We weren't sure the penguins were ready for someone like Donnie.

So he was in the Commvee back in the parking lot, and Darwin and I were the lucky ones in penguin suits.

Darwin moaned faintly. "I just hope nobody sees me in this getup."

Thanks to the mystical shaman who gave me the power to speak to animals, I was the only person in my family who understood his grumbling.

"Don't worry, Darwin," I told him. "My dad says they've closed off the sanctuary tonight, so it's just us here." I looked around as the sound of distant squawking started getting louder. "Us and about a thousand penguins, that is."

Up on the boardwalk Dad was practically hopping up and down as he peered at the penguins out at sea.

"Marianne, can you believe it?" he

gushed. "In moments we'll all be witnesses to the tender reunion between parent and child!"

All around us baby penguins began to pop up from burrows hidden in the sand. It was like a magic show, when the magician pulls a rabbit out of a hat. One minute you didn't see anything, the next. . .

Pop! Pop! Pop! Hundreds of little baby penguins jumped out of their snug burrows. They added their high little cries to the noise of their parents' hoarse calls.

"What's the big deal?" Debbie said, growling. "Didn't you say these dumb penguins do this every night?"

"Indeed they do, pumpkin," Dad said with a nod. "But each time it's like a little miracle when they find one another again amid the teeming multitude."

"Quiet down, everyone!" Mom said. "This time it's really for real. Eliza, put your penguin-camera on and make sure

Darwin's wearing his. And . . . action!"

Darwin and I crouched down in our penguin suits, watching the tiny babies that were starting to run up and down the beach, yelling, "Mommy! Daddy!"

A wave crashed on the shore and when the frothy, white foam slid back, hundreds of adult penguins struggled to their feet and waddled up the beach, calling to their chicks.

It was hard to believe any of the birds would ever find their own babies with all the noise and movement.

"Mawrgry!" yelled one penguin mother near me, calling the name of her baby.

"Mommy!" Somehow Baby Mawrgry heard the cry and rushed through the crowd to her mother. They met in a flurry of flapping wings. I made sure my penguin-cam was pointed that way.

"Wonderful, Eliza!" I heard my mother yell above the din while a penguin next to me was shrieking in my ear. "Grawdor! Get over here!"

"Yes, Daddy! As soon as this big penguin gets off my head," a muffled voice said from somewhere near my left foot.

"Ooops! Sorry," I said, hopping away from the opening to a well-hidden burrow.

"So you should be!" the father penguin said. He brushed sand off his baby, then asked, "Ready for dinner?"

The baby tilted back his head and opened his beak. I kept the camera focused on them, even when the father spit some food from his own throat into his son's beak.

"Eeeewww!" Debbie shrieked as she watched on the monitor. "Gross!"

"They don't have grocery bags, you know," I said, but Debbie probably didn't hear me because just then a roar went up from the hundreds of birds—a noise that was ten times louder than before.

"Something's wrong!" Darwin yelped.

All around us penguins started running about even more wildly. The penguins didn't seem to be looking for their families anymore, just someplace to hide. Parents lost their babies in the crowd as some birds rushed back to the water, and others dove into any nearby burrow. Most of the birds, though, just ran in circles.

I stared at the chaos on the beach. "What's happening?"

Chapter 2

Within seconds I saw what was causing all the commotion.

A pickup truck was tearing down the boardwalk. Many of the penguins had been wandering close to the walkway, hardly noticing my family. Now the penguins were running in fright from the roaring engine.

By the time the pickup truck screeched to a stop, the beach was almost empty. The babies were hidden again, but were afraid and calling to their parents. "Mommy! Daddy!"

I could see an incredibly tall, thin man uncurling himself from behind the wheel. "Nigel Thornberry! At last I found you!" he said, looking relieved.

"A-A-Are—are you nuts?" Mom choked out, glaring at him.

"Why? What do you mean?" The man looked around. For the first time, he seemed to notice the few birds still left on the beach. "Oh, no! I was sure I would get here long before the penguin parade!"

The man's whole body drooped, and he leaned against the boardwalk rail like a flower that had wilted. "My whole life is dedicated to preserving animals," he moaned. "Now look what I've done! I'm responsible for *another* disaster. Two in one day!"

I didn't know what else he'd done, but even I started to feel sorry for him.

"There, there, now." Dad patted the man on the back. "I'm sure it's not as bad as it looks . . . whatever it is."

While Dad tried to calm him down, Mom leaned over the rail, close to the spot where Darwin and I still stood.

"Eliza, maybe if you make those penguin cries again, you'll convince the other

birds it's safe to come back," she said. "They seem to think you're one of them. Those sounds you were making before sounded pretty authentic."

I gulped. The shaman had told me I wasn't supposed to ever let anyone know that I could talk to animals. If anyone found out, that would be the end of chatting with tigers and polar bears—and Darwin!

"Um, I was just copying their noises," I told Mom. "But I'll do the best I can."

I waddled along the water's edge, calling out to the penguins I could see swimming nervously just off shore.

"It's okay! He didn't mean to scare you!" I yelled in penguin talk.

One penguin, bolder than the rest, swam closer. I recognized her. It was Mawrgry's mother.

"We are not used to being hunted in this place, only by birds from the air and creatures in the sea," she said. "Are our babies not safe even here?"

I shook my head as best I could in my costume. "Nobody's going to hurt you or your babies," I said. "If you come out now, no one will scare you again, I promise."

Mawrgry's mother seemed to make up her mind that I was telling the truth. She swam bravely ashore, calling for her baby. Soon more penguin parents followed, and the reunion began all over again.

I knew I should have had my penguin-cam busy capturing all that, but I really wanted to know why the tall man needed to find my dad. So I focused on just a few families, like Mawrgry and her mom, then rushed back to the boardwalk. I had a feeling Mom would want more film, but I didn't want to miss a thing.

By the time Debbie dragged me onto the wooden planks, the man had perked up.

"See, it wasn't a disaster after all," my mother was saying, waving at the scene on the beach.

The man wiped his watery blue eyes and introduced himself as Lester Bovine. I noticed that his tanned face was almost as wrinkled as a crocodile's skin.

"I'm in charge of one of Australia's finest zoos," he boasted. But then he seemed to remember something, and his proud expression faded. "I arranged for the zoo to host a traveling exhibit of three spectacled bears, a rare species from South America."

Lester explained that the bears were almost extinct because they were hunted in their native country of Bolivia. In fact, they had been rescued from hunters who had trapped them illegally.

"This visit to Australia was to be the last stop for the traveling exhibit," Lester added. "The bears were due to be released into a sanctuary in Bolivia next week. But now—," Lester buried his face in his hands. "The plane crashed!" he groaned. "The one I hired to carry the bears back home."

"The plane *crashed?*" I exclaimed.

Dad twirled his mustache the way he did when he was worried. "Well, tell us what happened to the unfortunate pilot and the spectacled bears!"

Lester explained that the plane made a crash landing in New Zealand, in an uninhabited section of Urewera National Park. The pilot was unharmed, but by the time the rescue team got there, the bears had escaped from the damaged plane.

"Escaped?" Mom gasped. "You mean . . . they're roaming free in New Zealand right now? That's terrible!"

Lester seemed relieved that someone understood. "As I said, it could be a disaster and it's all my fault."

Dad looked anxious. "I say, there must be some way we can help."

Lester nodded happily. "That's why I came for you. I heard you were in Australia and realized you could help me."

"You're not expecting us to go on some kind of bear hunt, are you?" Debbie said, snickering.

"Exactly!" Lester flashed a toothy grin at her.

"You've *got* to be kidding me!" Debbie cried. "First penguins, now bears!"

But it was no joke. Lester told us he was going to fly out to New Zealand to search for the bears around the crash site. He wanted us to come too.

"By the time we get there, the bears could be anywhere," Mom pointed out.

Lester nodded. "But if you came to film the search and broadcast it on your show, that might focus attention on the bears," Lester said. "Perhaps other people will join the search then. It might be our only chance to find them."

My dad nodded too. "Sounds ripping! But everyone would have to agree. And Marianne and the girls were *so* looking forward to filming the penguins."

Mom was already packing her camera.

"Mom, do you really think we'll be able to find the bears?" I asked.

She grinned at me as she pulled the plug on the big TV monitor. "I certainly hope so, honey. Just imagine the kind of footage I could get."

I nodded. "I guess there aren't a lot of people who have even seen spectacled bears," I said, remembering that Lester had said they were really rare. "And I bet *no one* has ever seen spectacled bears that have crash-landed before."

Mom laughed. "And I know no one has seen bears in New Zealand," she added.

I could tell Mom was excited about the

chance to catch the bears—for real and on film. I was pretty excited too.

"Forget about the bears. Are there *people* in New Zealand?" Debbie asked. She was staring at a penguin regurgitating dinner for its baby. "Not penguins or other animals . . . PEOPLE!"

When Debbie heard that the island had plenty of people, plus luxury spas, she started to help Mom pack. "What are we waiting for?"

Darwin muttered in my ear, "Are we leaving? Does this mean we can get out of these monkey suits?" When I nodded, he gave a joyful chimp yelp.

"And what about you, Eliza?" Dad asked, turning to me.

"Let's find some bears!"

Chapter 3

Early the next morning I climbed up to the roof of the Commvee, our family's home.

"Ahoy, there!" I hailed my sister, who was stretched out on a lounge chair.

At that moment our family's vehicle was in seagoing mode, speeding through the Pacific Ocean on its way from Australia to New Zealand.

"Get out of my sun, twerp," Debbie muttered. Then she turned a page of the book she was reading. Wait a second. My sister was reading a *book?*

I couldn't remember the last time I'd seen my sister reading something that wasn't a glossy magazine with a rock star on the cover. Debbie's book actually had a kiwi—the bird, not the fruit—on the front.

"Whatcha reading?" I asked. "A book about New Zealand?"

"So?" Debbie said, shrugging.

Just then Dad popped his head over the railing. "So how are you getting on with that guidebook, pumpkin?" he asked Debbie while winking at me. "I hope you're not disappointed, Eliza, but I asked Debbie to represent our little 'tribe' during the ceremony where the traditional Maori warrior greeting is given. My trusty guidebook tells all about it, and Debbie will know just what to do."

"I don't mind," I said. "At least, I don't think I do. What are you talking about?"

Dad explained that Lester had arranged for a guide to lead us through the park where the plane had crashed. The guide's name was Tukaroto Porima. He was a Maori, from a tribe of people native to New Zealand.

"It seems Mr. Porima's home village performs Maori greeting ceremonies for visitors," Dad said. "It's a way for the

Maori to keep traditions alive. Mr. Porima has asked us to meet him there."

Visitors were always welcome, Dad told me, but were asked to choose someone to represent their group at the ceremony.

"Aren't you just thrilled, pumpkin?" he asked Debbie.

"Huh?" My sister barely lifted her nose from the book, but scribbled something on a pad beside her.

"I can see you're hard at work," Dad said gleefully. "I won't keep you!"

His head disappeared over the side of the Commvee.

"I can't believe it," I said, watching as she scribbled another note on the pad. "Debbie, I'm really impressed."

That's when I glanced down at Debbie's notepad. "Mud bath," it read, "one part warm mud plus ten parts water."

"Hey! That's a recipe for some beauty treatment," I said.

Debbie glanced up and sighed wearily. "Dad gave me this boring book to look at. I was going to use it as a footrest, when I noticed this section on the beauty secrets of New Zealand spas."

"You thought a penguin gagging was gross," I reminded her. "Taking a bath in mud sounds pretty disgusting."

"Not just *any* mud," Debbie said defensively. "It's a kind of beauty mud found in just a few places in the world." She frowned. "And I *have* to find some."

This time I was the one who shrugged. "Whatever."

I left Debbie to her reading and headed down to talk to Mom, who was steering the Commvee.

"Mom, why did you say it was terrible that those bears were loose on the island?" I asked. "Lester said the zoo was going to let the bears loose after they got home, so what difference does it make?"

"Because New Zealand is a special kind of place," she explained. "It's an island far away from any other land. Because of that, the animals there have lost their defenses against animals from other places. Many of the birds can't even fly! They've gotten used to living without predators."

I thought about that for a moment, then I understood. "You mean, if the bears stay there, they'll be a danger to animals that were never hunted before?"

Mom nodded. "If those bears mate, they could have babies and more babies. Soon they could overrun the island and make many species extinct."

"We've got to find those bears!" I said.

"And we've got to do it fast," Mom said. "Lester told me that one of those bears is about to have babies. If they're not found soon, we'll have more than three bears to worry about!"

Chapter 4

New Zealand is actually made of two big islands—North Island and South Island—and lots of tiny ones.

It was almost noon as my whole family stood at the gates of a Maori village on North Island. Lester Bovine looked like he might jump out of his skin if we didn't start looking for his lost bears right away.

"I understand the problem and will help you just as soon as the ceremony is over," said Tukaroto Porima, our guide. His village was located close to Urewera National Park, the big nature preserve where the plane had crashed.

Tukaroto led us past a corral of tall emus—ostrichlike birds—and through the wooden gates of the village. "I will enjoy introducing you to my Maori culture."

I'd already noticed one thing about

Maori culture. Like some of the other men, Tukaroto had curly patterns tattooed on his face. The tattoos swirled around his cheeks, nose, forehead, and chin.

He glanced at Donnie, who was jumping up and down and making faces at the emu.

"Eeeebeebabooooo!" Donnie yelled.

Tukaroto scratched his head, looking a little puzzled. "I see your family has customs that are different from those of the Maori. It is good to have a chance to meet and share our traditions."

I nodded, even though I wasn't certain anyone had the same customs as Donnie.

"And which of your family has been chosen to act as your representative?" Tukaroto asked my dad. "Every group today will perform some part of the *Powhiri*, our welcoming ceremony."

Dad proudly pushed Debbie forward. "Our Deborah here has been reading all about it," he said. "So no need for long explanations!"

But from the look on her face, I had a feeling Debbie was wishing she'd read more about greeting rituals and less about mud baths.

Just then a loud call came ringing out across the village. It was one of the Maori women singing out a welcome.

"That's the *karanga.* Now the age-old ceremony of greeting begins!" Dad told us. Next, a Maori man dressed like a warrior threw down a spearlike dart as a challenge to the *manuhiri*—the Maori word for visitors like us.

"What does that mean, Eliza?" Darwin asked, half-hidden behind me and looking anxiously at the dart. "They're not going to use us for shish kebabs, are they?"

I had read a little of Dad's guidebook, so I knew the dart-throwing was an old custom.

"Don't worry, Darwin," I whispered. "It's all part of the ceremony. See, a long time ago, visitors would show they wanted to be friendly by the way they acted when the dart was thrown."

A man from another group of visitors picked up the dart to show that we all came in peace.

Next, there were chants and dances that told the history of the Maori. Mom filmed it all.

"Now it's your turn, Deborah," Dad said to Debbie. He shooed her toward the front. "It's time for the *hongi*."

"Okay, okay, I'm going," Debbie grumbled. Then she spotted a teenage boy in the crowd of Maori. I could practically hear her cute-guy radar go off.

"I mean, gosh, this is great!" she suddenly gushed. Debbie flipped her hair back and sashayed to the front.

"It is time for the *hongi*," Tukaroto

announced, stepping forward. "The traditional Maori greeting."

"Oh, gotcha!" Debbie stuck out her hand. "Um . . . like, it's nice to meet you?"

Tukaroto frowned, shook his head, then moved closer to Debbie and leaned over, like he was going to kiss her on the nose.

"Huh?" Debbie backed up. Tukaroto just looked confused and followed her. So, Debbie backed up some more. Pretty soon it looked like they were doing some kind of weird dance around the village.

Finally Tukaroto stopped and threw up his hands. "I give up!" he growled. "The *hongi* has been refused."

"Oh, Debbie!" Mom lowered her camera and shook her head sadly at my sister. "Now you've offended them."

"What did I do wrong?" Debbie gulped. She looked around anxiously as the Maori started muttering angrily, including the boy she liked.

Suddenly Dad stepped in front of Debbie. "No, the *hongi* has NOT been refused!" he declared. "I will represent the *manuhiri.*"

Tukaroto smiled and took a step forward. Then he pressed his nose and forehead against Dad's for a minute before stepping back.

Dad flashed a big smile.

"That's *it?*" Debbie muttered. "I could have done that."

I sighed, glad that our hosts weren't mad at us. But a group of Maori men started to march toward us with determined looks on their faces.

"Now what?" I asked.

"Eliza, what are they carrying?" Darwin asked, covering his eyes.

"Knives," I gulped. "Great big ones."

Chapter 5

We didn't get chopped to pieces. But I was a little worried for a minute there.

It turned out the men were carrying knives because they were wood-carvers. Maori artists are famous for their wood carvings.

"You have the perfect profile for our latest totem," one of the carvers told my dad. "We must capture that face!"

Dad turned beet red behind his mustache, but looked flattered.

"Well, er, why, I couldn't, that is . . ." He looked at Mom, who shook her head.

"No, you couldn't," she said. "The bears, Nigel."

One of the men held up a camera. "We know you must leave soon to search for the bears, so if you would pose for just one moment. . . ."

Dad agreed to pose. I think he and Mom wanted to make up for Debbie's mistake with the greeting. While that was happening, I wandered outside the gates with Donnie and Darwin to talk with the emu.

The big birds were so surprised to hear me talk in their language, they forgot to be afraid.

"A human who speaks our tongue?" one said, edging closer to the rail. "Next I will see a mountain move."

We laughed together, but then the emu looked past my shoulder and skittishly moved away. I turned around to see that the Maori boy Debbie liked was standing right behind me. I hadn't heard him come up and hoped he hadn't heard me speaking Emu.

"Tena Koe," he said in Maori, waving a hand in greeting. "In case you didn't know, that means 'hi'."

"Hi," I said. "That means . . . well . . . hi."

He laughed. "My name's John. What's yours?"

"Eliza," I said. "And this is Donnie."

"Addabookee," Donnie said, turning a cartwheel. "And Darwin," I added.

"I see that you are friends with many animals," John said, looking at me, and then at Darwin, with a funny expression. "I saw you with the emu. Usually they do not let strangers come so close. You must have a special manner that animals trust."

"I guess so," I said nervously.

"Eliza!" It was Mom, waving to me from the Commvee.

"Oh, gotta go!" I told John. "Bye!"

But when I reached the Commvee, John was right behind me. It turned out he was Tukaroto's son, and was coming along on the search for the spectacled bears.

Suddenly my sister materialized beside me. "Hi, I'm Debbie," she said to John, flipping her hair. "Maybe we could be, like, bear buddies or something?"

John frowned a little then seemed to force a smile. "Thank you, Miss Deborah Thornberry, but . . . I do not think so, no."

I had a feeling he was still maybe a little mad about the way Debbie had treated his dad during the *Powhiri* ceremony.

"Big deal," Debbie muttered, but I could tell she still liked him by the way her ears turned red.

After that, John just ignored Debbie, and we all climbed aboard the Commvee.

"Let's get moving!" Lester snapped. "No time for flirting. We haven't a moment to lose!"

Chapter 6

"Are we almost there?" Darwin whined for maybe the twentieth time. "You know, chimps weren't built for hiking."

"It's not far now," I said. "Lester said it's just over that ridge."

We were tramping through Urewera National Park, up one of its small mountains. The trees grew really close to one another, and it was hard to find the path through all the scrubby bushes.

"I've never seen some of these things before," I marveled, watching a wingless cricket hide under a leaf as we approached.

As I stared at a strange-looking tree just ahead, John stopped in front of me.

"That is the *rata*," he said. "It grows around the other trees and sends its roots down to the earth." He pointed to where the roots of the *rata* seemed to trap the trunk of another tree in a cage. "It is something you will only see in New Zealand."

"That's, like, so cool!" Debbie said, pushing past me to be near John. "Oooh, and what's that?" She pointed at a chicken-sized bird sitting under a tall tree.

John rolled his eyes. "That's the kiwi. Our national bird."

"Remember, it was on the cover of that book you were reading," I told her.

Debbie ignored me. "Hey! Wait up!" she said, chasing after John up the trail.

"It's about time," I said to Darwin as soon as we were alone. "John's nice, but he's been hanging around me ever since we got to the park. I thought I'd never get a chance to talk to some of the locals." I waved toward the kiwi.

"What's so exciting about chatting with some silly bird?" Darwin whined.

"Well, I've never met a kiwi before." I called to the bird. "Hi, there! My name's Eliza."

"And my name is Hia Moe. But you can just call me Little Moe." The fat little bird tilted her head and blinked sleepily up at me. I noticed she had catlike whiskers and that there were nostrils all the way on the end of her long, skinny beak.

"I bet you use your beak to sniff out bugs, huh?" I said.

Little Moe nodded. "Delicious!"

Darwin shuddered. "Eliza, shouldn't we hurry and catch up with everyone?" he asked. "I don't want to get lost out here." He looked around the woods nervously and let out a startled squeal when a cricket hopped near his foot.

I nodded but figured the kiwi might be able to help us. "Did you by any chance see a bear around here?" I asked her.

"What is a . . . bear?" Little Moe asked.

"The kind we're looking for are about this tall," I said, tapping the top of my head. "And they have rings around their

41

eyes that look like my glasses."

"So, you are a bear?" Little Moe asked brightly.

"Well, no," I said. "Bears are shaggy and have claws and—"

"Claws?!" Little Moe's feathers suddenly ruffled, making them look even more like fur. "What do these bears eat?" she asked suspiciously.

"Um . . . fruits and leaves and a variety of, um, small animals," I said, "like mice and rabbits and, um . . . birds—"

"Ay!" Little Moe squawked. "That must have been what woke me up," she went on. "Normally, I sleep during the day, but there's been such commotion in the woods today."

She looked around nervously.

"Well, when you see one of them, just take off—," I advised, then caught myself as the kiwi flapped her stubby wings.

"Flightless, aren't I?" she said sarcastically. "We kiwi never needed to fly before you long-legs came here with your great shaggy beasts."

Before I could say anything else, John appeared on the path ahead. His eyebrows were raised as he looked at me and then at the kiwi. "That's funny. I could swear I heard *two* kiwi here a moment ago."

I tried to look surprised. "They *are* the national bird, right? I guess they must be everywhere."

"Well, we are almost at the crash site, so let's hurry," he said, frowning.

I nodded and followed him.

I was going to have to be careful while John was around with his sharp eyes and ears—very careful.

Chapter 7

"There it is! The plane! The plane!" Lester shrieked.

"And there, in a dramatic yet silent monument to the skill of the able pilot who piloted it to this unlikely landing site, is the lost aircraft," Dad was narrating as Mom filmed the wrecked plane.

It did look pretty dramatic. The wings were all bent and broken where they had hit the trees, and there was a huge hole in one side of the plane where a wing was pulled almost all the way off.

Dad pointed at the hole. "And in there are three empty cages, all that remains to show that, once, the rare spectacled bears were passengers on this fateful flight. But of course, it's too dangerous for us to venture inside—I say, Donnie, my boy!"

Dad forgot about the camera when he

saw Donnie rush up onto the broken wing and through the hole of the plane.

"Gibbeewangooen," Donnie's voice echoed inside.

"Nigel! Goodness knows what it's like in there," Mom said, lowering her camera and looking anxiously after Donnie.

"Oooobergerinher," came the sound of Donnie's happy chant.

"I'll have him back in a jiff, my dear," Dad said reassuringly, climbing up the wing. "I'm sure the boy . . . ooof . . . will be quite all right . . . uuuhh . . ."

We waited outside, and soon heard Dad's voice echo loudly through the plane. "You'll never guess—it's simply smashing! Our Donnie found a bear."

A few minutes later Tukaroto, Dad, and Lester gently led a small, frightened-looking bear out of the plane. Dad described how the bear had been found shivering inside one of the broken cages.

"Well, that wasn't very hard," Debbie said with a yawn. Then remembering that John was listening, she said, "I mean . . . this is so intense!"

"But I thought there were no bears here when the rescue party came for the pilot," I said to Tukaroto.

"It must have been frightened to find itself in a strange place," Tukaroto explained. "I believe it returned after the search party left with the pilot."

I moved closer for a look. The bear seemed young, maybe just a year old. It was a little smaller than Darwin and me. It had mostly dark fur, except for a yellowish-white patch in the shape of a little bib. The lighter patch spread up over the bear's face and around its eyes, like a big pair of funny-looking glasses.

"It's so cute!" Debbie said in surprise as she also took a closer look.

"It could still hurt you if you scared it,"

Mom cautioned. "Remember, those are claws it's got there." But the bear sat quietly while Lester slipped on a special harness. The harness wouldn't hurt the bear, and would make it easier to lead it back to the Commvee.

"Now, I suggest we divide into groups," Tukaroto said. "Lester will need to take the bear back to the Thornberrys' vehicle."

Lester gulped and looked around at the trees. "Alone?"

Tukaroto shook his head. "John will go with you—he knows his way in the forest. The rest of us will split up to look for the two bears that are left."

"Um, I'll go back too!" Debbie volunteered. "They'll need help with the bear." I'd bet she was more than just tired of tramping through the forest. She batted her eyes at John, who just groaned.

But Mom had another plan. "Good idea, Debbie, but I think Eliza should go," she said. "She seems to have a way with animals. You can come with me."

"But—," Debbie started to say.

"It will be much more 'intense' staying out and searching for the other bears," Mom said, winking at me. "But we'll need a guide through the forest."

"There we are then," Dad said happily. "Mr. Porima can go with you, my dear. I have an innate sense of direction, so I don't need a guide. And Donnie will come with me."

Mom didn't look so sure, but finally hoisted her camera and left with Debbie and Tukaroto. Dad and Donnie headed off down another trail.

"Thank goodness we're on our way back to civilization," Darwin said as we walked slightly behind John and Lester, who were too busy with the bear to pay any attention to us. By civilization, Darwin meant snacks.

"Before we get back, do me a favor," I whispered.

Darwin looked at me in alarm. "Whenever you say that, I end up in a cooking pot or someplace equally distressing.

"Nothing so bad this time," I assured him. "I just need you to make a scene."

"Huh?"

I explained that I wanted a few minutes alone to talk to the bear and get some clues about where the other bears might have gone. So I needed Darwin to lure Lester and John away for a few minutes.

"Well, what kind of a scene?" Darwin whined. "I'm no good at this secret agent kind of thing, you know."

I looked around for inspiration and spotted a fat cricket.

"Here!" I said, gently picking up the cricket and handing it to a squeamish Darwin. "Drop this on Lester's head—only, don't hurt it!"

Darwin nodded and slipped into the trees above us. A minute later Lester gave a high-pitched scream. "Arrrrgghhh!" Lester went racing off the trail into the bushes, yelling at the top of his lungs. "Arrrgghhh!"

"You'd better get him," I told John. "I'll watch the bear!"

John ran off after Lester.

"I quite enjoyed that, Eliza," Darwin said as he climbed back down.

I quickly introduced myself and Darwin to the spectacled bear.

"I am called Anillo by the ones who feed me," the bear said in a pleasant growly voice.

I explained that we were looking for the other bears and that they would all be free once they returned home to Bolivia.

Anillo looked sad. "That would be my wish, but we are not safe there."

"But now you will be," I told him, and

explained about the plan to release all the bears in a protected reserve.

Anillo cheered up when he heard that. But then he warned, "It will not be so easy to find the others.

"Caza is even smaller than me, but she loves to eat. She will go far to find food" — Anillo licked his snout—"but first she will look for water to quench her thirst."

"Water! Of course!" I said.

"As for the other," Anillo continued, "that is Lanuda. She will be looking for a place to hide herself and her cubs when they are born. It is almost her time."

"That's why we have to find her! Or else these woods will be filled with bears."

"That would not be a bad thing," Anillo said. "Those of our kind are few now."

I understood, but I also knew other animals would disappear if the bears stayed here. Luckily, these bears would be protected in a preserve when they went home.

Just then John returned, leading Lester.

"It seemed to come from out of nowhere," Lester was saying, looking anxiously up at the trees.

I looked up at the trees too, just so Lester and John wouldn't see me giggling. Darwin scratched his armpit, trying to look innocent.

John stared curiously at me again as we continued our trip down the trail.

Once Anillo was safe in the Commvee, Lester used the short-wave radio to report in to his zoo.

Meanwhile John prowled through the nearby bush to look for some leaves for Anillo to eat while I stayed in the Commvee to make a snack for Darwin, who was loudly complaining that wild animals got all the attention.

Then we went back outside and sat on the ground, munching on some peanut-butter-and-jelly sandwiches.

"Hey, whatcha got there, long-legs?"

I looked around and spotted the kiwi.

"What are you still doing up?"

"It's like I said before, you can't catch a wink of sleep around here today," Little Moe said. "I figured it might be quieter by the lake, but nooooooo. Everybody's in a tizzy over there because something's been poking around in the nests."

"What kind of something?" I asked, even though I had a pretty good idea.

The kiwi shrugged. "Don't know. Now, could I have some of that?"

I fed some crusts to the bird just as John came back. He watched the kiwi run for cover, and gave me a curious stare.

"I have an idea," I said, trying to distract him. "I figure the bears will be thirsty by now and will be looking for water. So let's check by a lake or something."

But John shook his head. "We should look along the trail. If the animals are not familiar with this place, they may stay close to the plane, as the other bear did."

"But that's not where they are!" I suddenly blurted.

John frowned. "And how do you know that? You think you know this forest better than me, who has lived here all my life? Just because you have a 'way with animals'?"

"Maybe I do know more about these bears than you do," I snapped.

"And maybe I know more about this forest than you do!" he growled back.

Then he marched off toward the woods, looking over his shoulder to shout, "You go your way—I go mine!"

And before I could say another word, he was gone.

Chapter 8

It took a while to persuade Lester that we should search by some water. But after John didn't come back right away, Lester agreed to head for a nearby lake with Darwin and me.

It took longer to persuade Darwin to come. I finally had to put the last of the peanut-butter-and-jelly sandwiches and two huge handfuls of Cheese Munchies into my backpack and start walking off.

"Now, Eliza, that's not fair!" he said, following me.

After only a few minutes I figured out it was a mistake to let Lester lead the way.

"Didn't we pass that tree before?" I asked, pointing to an especially fat kauri tree. "I remember that broken branch."

I remembered because Darwin broke it climbing away from a spider—one of the deadliest spiders in the world.

"Don't be silly!" Lester said. "I know exactly where I'm going."

I would have believed him more if he wasn't holding the map upside down.

"Maybe I'd better steer," I said, reaching for the map. But Lester just stamped his foot.

Unfortunately, that shifted some leaves, and we found out where Darwin's deadly spider had been hiding. As soon as Lester spotted it crawling near his boot, he went running off into the woods, yelling at the top of his lungs, "Spider! Aaaaaagggghhh!"

Darwin went running in the opposite direction. I was right behind him.

"Darwin! Slow down!" I called. "We're far enough away now."

"Wh-Wh-What?" Darwin stopped and clutched my arm. "Are you sure, Eliza?"

I nodded. "But I think we lost Lester."

At that moment a crowd of birds flew

overhead, screeching loudly. "Hide your eggs! Hide your eggs! The beast is loose!"

"It's the spider!" Darwin shrieked.

I shook my head. "No, birds eat bugs, remember? I think it's something else."

I looked back the way the birds had come. "Quick, Darwin! That way!"

A few minutes later we arrived at a place where the trees ended by the side of a clear, blue lake.

"Oh, no! Look at that poor duck!" I pointed to a bright orange duck that was limping by the side of the lake, dragging its wing. "She's broken her wing!"

But when I went over to help, the bird suddenly took flight—her wing was working perfectly.

"What a faker," Darwin said as we watched it swoop back to the spot we'd been. "I thought none of the birds here could fly."

"Only some of them can't. And I think

the reason she was faking was because she's protecting her eggs," I said. "She was just trying to lead us away from her nest."

I spoke softly to the nervous duck. "Don't worry, we're not after your eggs."

"You come any closer and I'll give you a taste of my beak," she said, ignoring what I'd said. The duck snapped her beak a couple of times to show she meant business.

"Uh, maybe we better leave," Darwin said.

"Look, we're just trying to track down the bears that are loose in these woods," I tried to explain. "We want to take them far away, where they won't hurt your babies."

"Bears?" I could see the duck was puzzled, so I made a movement like I was waving some claws.

"That horrid, shaggy thing?" she asked. "It was sniffing round here just a little while ago. But I tricked it, I did!"

She looked back toward the trees. "I think it's hiding somewhere over there."

"I don't like this, Eliza," Darwin muttered. "Now there's just the two of us and two bears out there. What if they're in the mood for a chimp entree after an appetizer of duck eggs?"

"Don't worry," I said. "Spectacled bears are more likely to run away than chase a human, and I don't think they're used to eating chimps. But I bet they're hungry. I wish we had something they *would* like to eat, but there's noth—"

I suddenly stopped. Darwin could tell I had an idea. And I could tell he didn't like it.

"No, Eliza! Anything but that!"

Chapter 7

"Do you really think this will work?" Darwin grumbled from his perch high in a tree. "Because a Cheese Munchie is a terrible thing to waste."

I didn't bother to reply. I was too busy dropping the cheesy snacks along the trail, hoping to lure at least one of the bears to the Commvee that way.

"Are you sure this is the right direction?" I called up to Darwin. We'd figured out that the easiest way to find our way through the woods was to use Darwin's bird's-eye view.

"It's not far now!" he yelled. "Just keep going." He climbed back down and absently picked up a Cheese Munchie.

"Hey, stop that! You're eating our bear bait," I said, holding up a golden nugget. "This is the last one."

I was hoping that a hungry bear would sniff out and follow the trail of Cheese Munchies, but now we wouldn't have enough left to lead it all the way back to the Commvee.

"I guess your plan won't work after all," Darwin said cheerfully. "I'd better eat them."

I couldn't think what to do next.

"Tena Koe!"

Darwin and I both whirled around at the sound of the greeting. I must have looked pretty silly holding up a Cheese Munchie and looking so surprised, because John burst out laughing.

I did too. After that, it was easy to forget we'd ever fought.

"Tena Koe," I replied. Then I explained about the bear bait.

"Good idea," he said, "just like your idea of looking by the lake. You were right."

I smiled at him and shrugged. "And you

were right about not knowing our way in the forest." I told him about losing Lester.

"We should look for him," John said. "But first, let's complete your trap."

"It's a lure," I corrected him. "But I've run out of bait. And we're still far from the Commvee," I said.

John frowned. Then he grinned. "We will just have to make another kind of trap. One that will hold the bear here, without harming it, while we go back for a harness, since Lester ran off with the one we had."

John explained that his grandfather had taught him how to make a trap for small animals. He said he was sure he could figure out a way to make it safe for the bear. So we made a bigger one, using sturdy branches that had fallen from trees nearby. Even Darwin helped, in exchange for the last Cheese Munchie.

"If we cover it with leaves and grass, it will look like a hollow log or something and not so much like a trap," I suggested.

Once the bear went into our bear-friendly trap, John would pull a string made from our shoelaces and an old yo-yo from my backpack. The string pulled a latch that made the door swing shut.

After that we would just need to wedge a big stick against the door. The bear would be stuck inside.

"But perhaps it will claw its way out," John said, looking doubtfully at our stick structure when we were done.

I shook my head. "I'm sure it will hold it long enough for us to go get some help," I said. Secretly, I was hoping to have a chance to talk to the bear and convince it to stay inside the trap until we got back. But I couldn't tell that to John!

"Now for the bait," I said, dramatically reaching into my backpack to pull out the slightly squished peanut-butter-and-jelly sandwich.

I placed the sandwich inside the trap, on a bed of rustly leaves. Their noise would tell us when the bear was inside.

"We're ready," John said. We all hurried to hide in the bushes. John covered the telltale string with some leaves.

"Now we wait," I said.

We didn't have to wait long. There was the noise of a twig breaking and the padding of bare paws in the dirt. Then we heard a loud sniffing sound and a grunt.

"Almost there . . . ," John whispered. Then came the noise we'd been waiting for as something stirred the leaves inside the trap.

"Now!" I yelled, and John pulled the string. We rushed out and John quickly jammed a stick in place against the trap-door, wedging it shut.

"We've got the bear!" I shouted.

Chapter 10

Only it wasn't the bear. It was Donnie.

We got the trapdoor open before he was able to take a bite of the sandwich.

"Neebooobunner!" he pleaded as I tried to take it away from him.

"No, Donnie, we need it," I said. "Not that our idea will work now that you've eaten our trail." The Cheese Munchies were all gone from the path.

In a flash something shaggy dropped down from a nearby tree and rushed into the trap to snatch the sandwich from Donnie's hand. Donnie was so surprised that he sprang out of the trap and started yelling, "Beeyoodegahgah!"

"It's the bear!" Darwin shrieked, running around in circles, waving his arms. "Help! Help, Eliza! After that sandwich, it'll come after me!"

Then Darwin raced up into a nearby tree, followed by Donnie, who must have thought it was all a game.

"It *is* the bear!" I shouted to John. "Really, this time!"

John moved like lightning. We had already pulled the string when Donnie was in the trap, so John reached inside for the door and banged it shut. The bear was too busy growling over the sandwich to notice. I quickly pushed the branch across the door again to jam it closed.

The bear finally looked up.

"Get another branch," I told John. "We might need it. Hurry!"

He dashed away and I stepped closer to the trap.

"Listen," I said to the surprised bear. "My name is Eliza. You're Caza, right? Don't worry, we're your friends."

Caza looked at me suspiciously. "Would a friend trap me in such a way?"

"I absolutely, positively promise we'll let you go," I told her. As fast as I could, I explained about the sanctuary in Bolivia.

"But I am happy here," Caza said. "The food in this place is like none I have tasted before." She licked some peanut butter off her snout.

I assured Caza that there would be plenty of food where she was going.

By the time John got back, Caza was curled up, ready for a nap. She'd promised to wait quietly until we could return with a harness.

"The trap worked better than I expected," John said, looking at the sleepy bear. "She's not even trying to get out."

He suggested we hurry back to the Commvee for one of the harnesses. I knew I could lead Caza back without one but John would be suspicious if I did.

That's when we heard some more rustling in the bush.

"Uh-oh, there's no room for two bears in there," was all I had time to say, before a familiar face poked out from between two bushes.

"I say, have you seen Donnie?" asked my dad as he stepped out from the forest. "I seem to have lost the lad."

"Dad, what are you doing here?"

"I appear to have lost my way." Dad scratched his head. "How extraordinary—because I do have an innate sense of direction, as you know."

Luckily, Dad was carrying one of the bear harnesses, so we were able to lead Caza back to the Commvee right away. I asked to hold the leash because I knew it would make Caza feel safer.

John led us back to the Commvee. His father was right. John sure knew the park inside and out. I was especially glad he knew his way *out*!

"Come in, Thornberrys," a voice called

from the radio as we got Caza settled in the Commvee with Anillo.

Dad listened for a minute. "Lester was found by some hikers," he reported. "I wonder how he came to wander so far away? Well, he managed to contact Debbie, your mother, and Tukaroto, so we'll take the Commvee and meet them now. And guess what?"

"What?" I asked.

Dad's eyes twinkled. "Lester has found the last bear!"

"Well, I don't exactly *have* the bear, but I think I have a lead," Lester admitted when we were all together again.

"Where is it?" I asked.

But before Lester could tell us, he insisted on telling us about how he'd been found on the trail by some tourists.

"Not that I was ever *really* lost, you

understand," he said. He glanced at me, then quickly looked away. "It's just that, in trying to lure the spider away from Eliza, I wandered off the path and my map was . . . er . . . a bit backward."

"Upside down, he means," I muttered.

"As I was saying," Lester said, clearing his throat. He went on to explain that the tourists who had found him were part of a bigger group. When they'd met up with the rest of their party, some of them were talking about seeing a yeti.

"A yeti?" Tukaroto looked puzzled.

"It's a mythical beast some believe roam the wilds of America," Dad started to explain. "Some call it the abominable snowman, others call it—"

"It looks like a bear," Mom told Tukaroto.

"Ah!" Tukaroto understood at once. "Our missing mother-to-be."

"Where'd the bear go?" I asked Lester.

It turned out the tourists had seen it

climb into the back of a camper when a family was tossing out some garbage. Before anyone could warn them, the family climbed in themselves and drove off.

"But where are they now?" John asked.

"Someone overheard them arguing about where to go next," Lester said. "Apparently, they couldn't decide whether to visit the thermal springs and mud pools, the Maori village, or the glowworm grotto."

We all looked at one another. Which should we try first?

Suddenly Debbie spoke up. "That thermal place!" she said, folding her arms. "The one with the mud."

No one else had a better idea, so everyone piled into the Commvee and before long we arrived at the thermal springs.

Chapter 11

"Whakarewarewa," I said, reading the sign as we drove through the entrance.

"It is Maori," Tukaroto told us. "From *te whakarewarewatuga-o-te-ope-a wainiao.*"

"It means 'the uprising of the war party at Wainino,'" John said. "In the old days Maori warriors did a war dance before a great battle at the geyser here. It was thought to be a sacred place."

"Geysers?" Debbie frowned. "I thought it was a spa, with mud pools."

Tukaroto laughed. "You will find mud here, yes, but no one would bathe in it."

Debbie turned away in a huff. I was the only one who heard her mutter, "That's what you think!"

Tukaroto told us that, once again, we needed to split up.

"This time, I think you should go with

Tukaroto," Mom said quickly, looking at Dad. "I think the two of you will cover more ground when you're together."

"Splendid thinking!" Dad flashed a big grin and went off happily with Tukaroto.

"Um . . . this way, Mr. Thornberry," Tukaroto said, gently leading my father away from the crumbling edges of a steaming mineral pond.

Debbie made goo-goo eyes at John, who quickly volunteered to go with Mom.

So that left me and the three D's— Debbie, Donnie, and Darwin.

"Debbie, I'm leaving you in charge here," Mom said, asking us to check around the campers in the parking lot first, to see if there was any sign of a bear.

My sister was sulking over not being allowed to go with John, but she nodded.

"And stay together," Mom warned, as she walked off with John.

It took us only a little while to hunt

around all the campers. Most of them were locked, so all we could do was knock and wait for a bear to answer. None did.

"Let's go see the geyser," I said.

Debbie dragged her feet, upset because it wasn't a spa after all. So that left me to chase after Donnie when he started to walk along the top of the low wall that lined the visitors' path like it was a tightrope.

"Hey! Stop that, Donnie!" I yelled, when he started picking the hats off tourists as he walked past their heads.

"Sorry! Sorry!" I said, replacing the caps and visors and sun hats. "Donnie, come down!"

Donnie shrugged and climbed down. Then he bowed as he presented a fishing cap back to its red-faced, bald owner.

I sighed with relief and stopped to read one of the signs posted along the path.

"Hey, Darwin, look at that," I said,

pointing at a boiling lake. "Can you believe how prehistoric this place looks? I bet it looked just the same when the dinosaurs were around."

But Darwin wasn't listening. "What's over there, Eliza?" he asked. A crowd of tourists had gathered in one spot.

"I don't know. Let's check it out."

Darwin and I pushed our way through the crowd to the front. "It's just a hole," Darwin said in disappointment.

But just then steam started leaking from the hole. And a moment later a jet of hot water erupted almost a hundred feet into the air like a spitting volcano.

"Yikes!" Darwin turned tail—literally— and ran off as the tourists oohed and ahhed over the geyser.

By the time I caught up with him, he had almost stopped shaking. "It's all right, Darwin, we'll just find Debbie and Donnie and head back to the Commvee," I said, trying to calm him down. "Now, where are those two?"

That's when I spotted Debbie far off down the path. She was about to climb up onto the wall. I could just see the smile on her face as she looked past it at a field of bubbling mud beyond. The goop looked so smooth and chocolatey, like it was a tub of delicious hot-fudge sauce. It even made me want to dive right in.

"What's she doing?" Darwin asked.

I knew just what Debbie was doing. She was looking for mud for her beauty bath.

I knew something else, too—something Debbie didn't, because she'd never really read Dad's guidebook.

"Debbie, don't!" I squeaked in horror.

I'd read all about that mud in the little sign by the fence. I knew the mud wasn't warm, like Debbie thought. It was hot. Really, really hot—hot enough to melt my big sister.

Chapter 12

"Debbie! Get away!" I screamed, running toward the wall. The crowded pathway was like an obstacle course of tourists.

Debbie didn't hear. She was sitting on top of the wall, ready to jump down to the mud pool.

I'd never make it in time to stop her!

"Hey! Watch it, dodo!" Debbie ducked as Donnie suddenly appeared on the wall beside her, waving a familiar-looking fishing cap by her head.

She took a swipe at it, but Donnie was too quick for her. Instead, he tossed it out over the wall into the mud pool.

I saw Debbie gasp in horror as the hat exploded in a poof of smoke almost before it landed.

A bubble of mud popped with a loud burp as I arrived, panting, beside Debbie.

"Thanks, Donnie," I heard her say in a tiny voice.

Donnie smiled at her angelically and burped, louder than the mud pool.

"Uh . . . Eliza, could you help me down now?" Debbie asked me in the same small voice. "I don't think I can move."

We were back at the Commvee when everyone else showed up.

"No sign of our bear," said Mom wearily.

"Where to next, poppets?" Dad asked. "Shall we see if our quarry has headed back to the village? Or set our sights on the fabulous caverns of the glowworm grotto?"

"Caverns?" The word made me remember something Anillo had told me about Lanuda looking for a dark den. "The grotto is a cave?"

Mom nodded. "Yes, honey. Why?"

"I bet that's where she is!" I gasped. "I mean . . . most bears like caves, right? And this one will be looking for a nice, safe den to have her babies. She's going to have them any minute. Let's get going!"

Chapter 13

A little while later we pulled in to the entrance to the glowworm grotto.

"The grotto closes in fifteen minutes," the woman at the entrance warned us. "Not many people are left in there now. Follow this road to the parking lot."

"But everyone seems to drive a camper," Mom sighed when we caught our first glimpse of the parking lot. "It will take us forever to check them all."

"Buck up, Marianne!" Dad said. "It may take us a while, but if we all . . ."

I looked at Dad as his voice trailed off, then followed his pointing finger.

The back door to one of the campers was hanging wide open. Scattered on the ground just outside it were torn candy wrappers and limp fruit rinds.

"My bear!" Lester cried.

He led the charge to the grotto. The light quickly faded behind us as we got deeper into the caves, fighting the swarm of tourists on their way out.

A few workers tried to convince us to turn back, since the last tour was over and the lights were shutting down. But my dad stayed behind to explain while we all went on ahead.

"This way!" I heard John's voice ahead of us in the darkness. We'd reached a section that was lit only by the eerie little lamps of thousands of tiny glowworms covering the cavern walls.

"Wow," I said. "This is so cool . . ."

"But so dark," Darwin muttered.

He was right. It was hard to spot anything but shadows as everyone stumbled around in the great cave.

Darwin and I inched away from the others until I knew we were hidden in the darkness.

"Lanuda!" I called softly. I explained in a whisper who I was and about the home waiting for her and her babies in Bolivia.

"I hear the bear! It's coming from over there!" I heard John say. Only it was me he heard.

I had to hurry. "Please! Where are you? Your cubs will be so much happier in a place where they can be safe," I said into the darkness, hoping that Lanuda could hear me.

"I've almost reached her," John's voice was closer now.

"Please answer me!" I begged.

"Do you promise?" Lanuda asked. I was surprised at how close she was. Her voice came from right beside me.

"I promise!" I said, just as a light started to fill the grotto.

"You will keep your promise, hairless one?" she asked again. Then I felt Lanuda nuzzle my hand, and I knew she wouldn't

fight us when we led her back to the Commvee.

Suddenly a bright light appeared. It was Dad, carrying a lantern and leading a bunch of workers with powerful flashlights of their own.

Lanuda let out a low growl.

"Careful, or you'll scare her," I warned everyone.

I pointed at the small spectacled bear half-hidden in a crevice in the wall. Two newborn cubs were curled at her feet, their eyes still sealed shut as they yawned.

Lanuda sniffed the air, then looked at me before turning back to lick her cubs.

"How did you find her in the dark?" John asked as we were leaving the cave, looking at me with that familiar funny expression.

I blinked at him behind my glasses. "The same way you did. I just followed the bear sounds."

Chapter 14

The plane got tinier and tinier in the blue sky. I waved until it was just a speck.

"Bye, bears!" I yelled up into the air.

Darwin rolled his eyes at me. "They can't hear you, you know."

"I know," I said. "But it's fun to yell anyway."

I'd already said my real good-byes to the bears when Lester took them to a nearby airfield. Tukaroto and John had gone home too.

"Hey, where is everyone?" I asked.

Darwin shrugged. "Your sister is taking that bubble bath she was talking about all morning," he reported.

"I guess it will be a while before she wants a mud bath again," I said. "And where's Donnie?"

Darwin shuddered. "The last time I saw

him, he was in the kitchen making some sort of Donnie-snack. Believe me, you don't want to go in there right now. I'm sure I saw bugs in that sandwich."

I knew Mom was behind the wheel of the Commvee, getting ready to leave.

Dad suddenly appeared with a big box. "Ah, Eliza," he said, flashing a grin. "I know you'll be tickled pink when you see what's inside this little box of mine.

"Why? What is it? A present?"

"You could say that," Dad said, beaming. "Go on, open it!"

"Do you think it's more Cheese Munchies?" Darwin whispered to me.

I flipped open the top of the carton, then let out a gasp.

I think Dad thought it was a gasp of joy, because if anything, his smile got wider.

But Darwin saw the cardboard wing of the penguin costume that flopped out of the box and gasped too.

"I knew you couldn't *bear* leaving before we finished our little documentary, Eliza," Dad said, snickering over his pun. "So I've told your mother to steer us back to the Australian beach, pumpkin."

I smiled weakly.

"Or should I say 'penguin'?" Dad laughed. "Ar, ar!"

"Arrrrrr, Arrrrr!" I replied, groaning. That's penguin for "Oh, no, not again!"

Discovery Facts

Australia: Located in the southern hemisphere, Australia is the smallest continent, but also one of the largest countries in the world.

Emu: The emu is the second largest bird species alive today, often growing to a height of more than five feet.

Kiwi: A small bird about the size of a chicken that is covered with thick, furlike feathers and tiny wings.

Maori: The Maori are a group of Polynesian people who first arrived in New Zealand in the twelfth century, four hundred years before Europeans reached the islands.

New Zealand: About the size of Colorado, New Zealand is a small country in the South Pacific.

Penguin: A marine bird that can't fly but can swim very quickly. Most penguins live in the southern hemisphere.

Spectacled Bear: This species of small, shaggy black bears is found in South American countries such as Peru, Ecuador, and Colombia, but mostly in the forests of the Andes mountains. It gets its name from the pale fur that circles its eyes.

Urewera National Park: This national park is located on the north island of New Zealand.

About the Author

Maria Rosado lives in Brooklyn, New York, but dreams of traveling far and wide like the Thornberrys—especially to New Zealand. Ever since she saw photographs of the little blue penguins, Maria has wanted to write a story about them. Now she has!

Maria is the author of many books and articles for children, including two other books featuring the Thornberrys. She lives with a patient husband, who enjoys watching *The Wild Thornberrys* with her, and a very fat cat who is a lot bigger than a fairy penguin.